Little Muslims
Grow and Learn Series

Let's learn about

Being Kind to Animals

All praise is due to Almighty Allah,
Lord of the Worlds,
the Most Merciful, Most Beneficent.

'O' you who believe! Seek help through patience and prayer.
Surely, Allah is with the patient.'

These books are dedicated to all the little Muslims in the world.
May Allah guide you and help you grow strong in faith.

- S.Z.R.

Little Muslims Books

Dear parents,
Little Muslims Grow and Learn books are designed to make reading a
wholesome and enriching activity for both parents and children.
Throughout the stories of life lessons, you will find questions,
discussion topics and relevant verses from the Holy Qur'an and/or
religious narrations pertaining to the specific story. Please utilize these
sidebars to help engage your children and allow them to understand
these stories better.

Once upon a time there was a boy named Amin. He lived in a big neighborhood with lots of houses and trees. Amin loved his neighborhood. He liked how all the trees provided shade during the hot summer days, and that all the leaves would turn pretty colors during the fall.

Usually around the trees Amin would see cats. Actually Amin saw a lot of cats in his neighborhood. He didn't have any pets, and he was a little scared of cats, but he always enjoyed watching them play with grass, leaves or small flowers.

One day Amin and his friend, Salman, were playing in Amin's front yard. They were practicing soccer. The weather was great – especially for playing outside. The sun was out, but the big oak tree in Amin's yard was giving the boys plenty of shade.

"Salman, try to block this shot!"

Amin dribbled the ball a few feet, and kicked the soccer ball through Salman's legs, and into the small net behind him.

"Goal!" yelled Amin, and he threw his hands up.

"Good shot!" said Salman. "You are getting better and better!"

"Thanks! I am trying to get my skills perfected before soccer season," said Amin.

"I am tired! Let's take a break," said Salman, and the boys sat down on the grass.

Amin went inside to get some juice, and when he came back he saw Salman looking at something on the ground.
"What is it?"

"I see this trail of ants," said Salman.

Then he got up and was about to step on them, when Amin stopped him.

"Wait!" said Amin. "Don't do that!"

"Why not?" asked Salman. "They're ants. They will just bite us."

"Well let's just sit somewhere else. They aren't climbing all over us, so let's just leave them alone."

Salman looked a bit confused. Everyone knew ants bite, and the bites hurt and itch a lot! Why would anyone want to help ants?

Question: Did you know that animals are also creations of Allah? Because of this, we are supposed to treat them kindly and not be harsh with them. We should treat all of Allah's creations with respect. Even plants and trees.

"You know my dad told me once that ants are Allah's creatures, too," said Amin. "Even though they can be annoying and bite us, they shouldn't be treated harshly. We shouldn't walk around trying to hurt them."

Amin and Salman talked about a time when they were in school and playing outside during recess, when they saw one of their classmates looking at a group of spiders. Instead of just leaving them alone or walking away, he started stepping on each one!

Amin remembered feeling really bad because the spiders were just insects – where else were they supposed to go?

Discuss: Allah says in the Holy Qur'an that we should be kind to all of His creations, big and small. In fact even an animal as small as an ant should not be treated badly just because we as humans are bigger. Prophet Sulaiman was known to be able to speak to and understand animals. In one famous story he tells his group of followers to be careful not to step on an ant as they walked on the ground, because he heard the chief of the ants telling all the ants to hide as they saw the group coming with Prophet Sulaiman. On this big Earth that Allah has created, He has made many creatures. We all have a purpose, from the smallest ant to the biggest elephant.

One day, while Amin was riding his bike in the neighborhood, he noticed a small group of older kids across the street laughing and pointing at a cat.

Amin rode his bike over to them and saw that there were a few boys who were bothering the cat by using a stick.

They would push the cat around with the stick, or poke its back. Amin could see the cat was clearly upset by the actions of the boys!

"I think the cat doesn't like what you all are doing," said Amin. "Why don't you all leave it alone?"

"Who cares? It's just a cat," laughed one of the boys.

"Yeah, what is it going to do? Jump on us?" said another boy.

"It might be just a small cat, but it has feelings, too," said Amin. "You shouldn't just bother another animal because you are bigger than it. That's not fair. What if someone kept bothering you for no reason – how would you feel?"

Question: Have you ever seen anyone bothering an animal? Did you do anything to stop them?

Discuss: Sometimes we think that just because an animal might be smaller than us that it is OK to bother them. But this is not fair in Allah's eyes. No matter how big or small, we should treat animals kindly, and take care of their needs. The Holy Prophet Mohammad (PBUH) has said that we should take care of animals in regards to their health and safety, and if we are riding them or using them, we should make sure to give them water and not make them too tired.

"I never thought of it that way," said one of the boys who was holding the stick. He dropped the stick and said to his friends, "Let's go play at the park."

After the boys left, Amin went to the cat and looked at it. He could tell the cat was very scared. Amin didn't like cats very much, but he wanted the cat to know that it was safe now.

"Go home now, go," said Amin to the cat. "It's OK, don't worry, I am not going to bother you."

Then Amin got back on his bike and rode home.

When Amin got home, his father and mother were waiting for him.

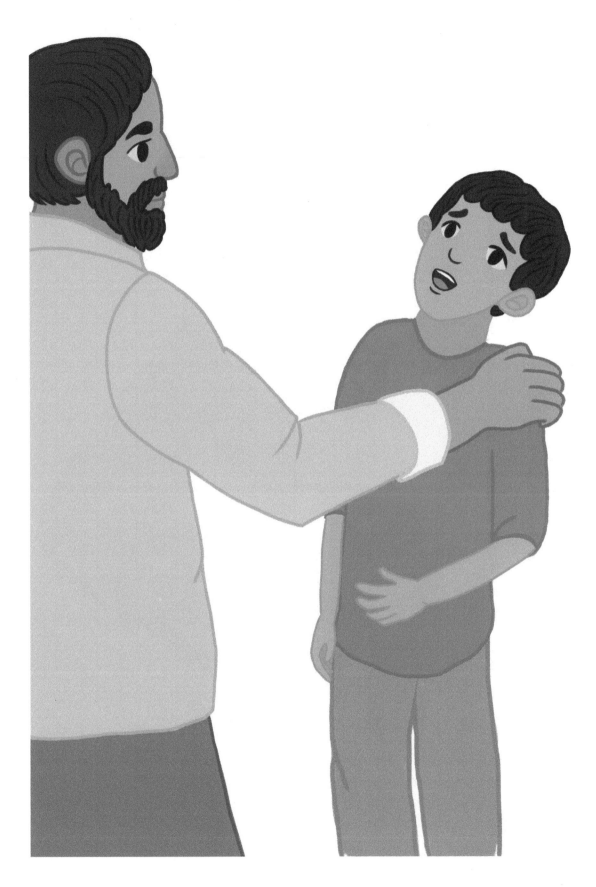

"Where have you been Amin?" asked his father. "You are late."

"I know, I'm sorry Dad. But there were some kids being a little mean to a cat, so I tried to help it," he said.

"Oh really?" said Amin's father. "What were they doing?"

"They were bothering the cat with a stick, so I told them that the cat looked scared and they shouldn't bother it just because they are bigger."

"That is really nice of you to do that Amin," said his dad. "It is important to take care of animals, especially when we see anyone bothering animals. You know there is a story of the Holy Prophet and how he was doing wudhu for prayers. While he was doing it, he saw a cat come by looking at the pot of water. He figured the cat was thirsty, and so he moved away and let the cat drink from the pot. Then he waited until the cat was finished to continue to do his wudhu. This teaches us that kindness to animals is important, as it shows we are being to kind to Allah's creatures."

There is a purpose for all of God's creations. Just because an animal might not be "bigger" or "smarter" than one of us doesn't mean we can treat it unfairly. On the other hand, this also does not mean that we can't kill any animals, for example when we kill animals to eat them. In the Holy Qur'an Allah has told us that He has created some animals for us to eat. It means that we should not bother or hurt animals for no reason. Even if we are killing an animal to eat, we are supposed to take care of it, and give it water first, and then kill it quickly, so the animal does not feel a lot of pain. Hurting one of Allah's creations for "fun," is a big sin, and if we see anyone doing this, we should stop them and remind them that all of Allah's creations deserve justice.

Let's talk more!

The Holy Qur'an talks about how the Earth is for all of Allah's creatures, big and small.

"There is not an animal that lives on the earth, nor a being that flies on its wings, but they form communities like you. Nothing have we omitted from the Book, and they all shall be gathered to their Lord in the end."
Surah Al-An'am, verse 38

"And the earth, He has assigned it to all living creatures."
Surah Rahman, verse 10

Narrations (Ahadith):

"Fear God with regard to animals. Ride them when they are fit to be ridden, and get off their backs when they are tired. Surely, there are rewards for being kind and gentle to animals, and for giving them water to drink."
-Prophet Mohammad (SAW)

Activities:

*<u>Learning about different animals</u> - Take a few moments to talk about different animals in the world, where they live, and what they do. This will help children understand more about these creatures of Allah.

*<u>Animals and where they live</u> - Kids can draw their favorite animals and a picture of their habitat. What does the animal like to eat? How does it sleep?